JULY 29, 2024
ALWAYS REMEMBER TO CHERISH THE
MOMENTS, WHILE YOU STILL CAN
Enjoy!

Elysia Varga

The Echo Of Saudade

Some love stories never die, even when they do

The automated analysis of the work in order to obtain information, in particular about patterns, trends and correlations in accordance with §44b UrhG ('Text and Data Mining') is prohibited.

© 2025 Elysia Vargas

Publisher: BoD · Books on Demand GmbH,
Überseering 33, 22297 Hamburg, bod@bod.de

Print: Libri Plureos GmbH,
Friedensallee 273, 22763 Hamburg

ISBN: 978-3-7693-3835-5

Dedicated to my mom, who always believed in this book.

Prologue

There are stories that time forgets, and others it preserves in soft whispers and faded letters, tucked between the pages of old books. This is one of the latter—a tale not often told aloud, but always felt in the quiet moments between heartbeats.

It begins with a girl named Amelia, and a sound—music, drifting from the chapel at dusk. It was not just melody; it was a calling. And when she followed it, she found Edward.

What unfolded between them was neither hurried nor planned. It was the kind of love that blooms in silence, unspoken but all-consuming. Yet, the world has little mercy for love that defies expectation. And so, what should have been a beginning became a battleground between longing and duty.

This is a story of beauty and sorrow, of hearts that met in perfect harmony, only to be pulled apart by the cold hands of fate. Amelia's future lies not with Edward, but elsewhere—bound to a name, a promise, and a life not her own.

What remains to be seen is whether love can survive in memory... or whether some music is meant only to be heard once.

Chapter 1: A Melody in the Wind

The village of Rosemoor was still slumbering under a blanket of morning mist. The first rays of dawn painted the rooftops in soft colours of gold, yellow and even a bit of orange while the air was filled with the scent of freshly-baked bread streaming out of the Hartley bakery.

Amelia Hartley stood at the window of her small bedroom, gazing out at the world as it was woken by the cozy warm sun. She watched as the mist slowly wiped away from the winding hills that surrounded the village, revealing the emerald green of the meadows beyond and the sun tickling her glass like skin. But her thoughts were elsewhere, drawn irresistibly to the abandoned chapel on the edge of town.

It was two weeks ago. That's when down at the chapel, she heard the mesmerizing melody for the first time.

The beautiful melody had flown through the air as she walked home from the market, each note pulling her heart with a certain familiarity. She had followed the sound, her feet moving without her permission, until she stood at the chapel's majestic doorway, taking a glimpse inside.

There, hunched over the dust-covered piano, was a man, which she had never seen before. His fingers glided over the keys with a delicacy, each movement filled with a passion that made her heart flutter. She had watched him for what felt like hours, mesmerized by the way his soul seemed to be one with the piano.

And now, every morning since, Amelia found herself at her window, hoping to hear that melody again. She knew it was foolish—silly, even—but something about that music, about that man, had carved them into her thoughts, lingering like an echo in her heart.

That day, she promised herself, she would go to the chapel again. She had to know more about the man who played with such grace and beauty. And maybe, she thought with butterflies in her stomach, she might even introduce herself.

The village was waking now. Below, she heard her father in the bakery, preparing loaves for the morning rush. The familiar sounds of the shop—clinking pans, the soft sound of her father's humming—were comforting, but today, they were overwhelmed by the pull of that distant chapel.

Amelia was sure. With a nervous flutter she said to herself: "I am going to the chapel. And this time, I won't just listen.

Chapter 2: Shadows in the Light

The bell above the bakery door rang softly as Amelia stepped down the stairs, signalling the arrival of the first customer of the day. She reached the bottom step just in time to see William Crawford step inside, his tall silhouette against the morning light that streamed through the open door.

William imbodied a fine gentleman—his dark hair neatly combed; his clothes perfectly tailored. His presence seemed to raise attention wherever he went, a fact he was well aware of. The villagers often spoke of him in quiet tones, not out of fear, but out of respect for his wealth and influence. As the owner of most of the land around Rosemoor, William Crawford held a certain power over the small community, a power that had long fascinated—but also frustrated—Amelia.

As Amelia hoped he had not yet seen her, she quietly snuck up the stairs again, but seconds later, she heard that deep yet soothing voice that she hated more than anything.
"Good morning, to you too Miss Hartley," the voice said.

Letting out a sigh she slowly came down the stairs. Wiliam greeted her with a warm, practiced smile as he removed his hat and stepped closer. "I assume you're well today?"

Amelia returned the smile, though it didn't quite seem to have reached her eyes.

"Good morning, Mr. Crawford. We're just opening up, but I'm sure my father can help you with whatever you need."

William's gaze lingered on her, a hint of possessiveness in his eyes. "Actually, I was hoping to speak with you, Amelia. May I have a moment of your time?"

She hesitated, as she glanced toward the back of the shop where her father was busy kneading dough. She knew what William wanted—he had been persistent in his intentions for months now, and while he had always been polite and respectful, there was an unspoken pressure behind his words that left her feeling uneasy and unsure.

"Of course," she replied, following him around the corner. They moved to a small table near the window, where the sunlight fell in through lace curtains, casting patterns onto the wooden table.

William gently pulled the chair for Amelia, before also sitting down, his hands folded neatly on the table. He studied her for a moment, as if searching for the right words. As if he hadn't done a thousand times already.

"Amelia," he began, his voice low and controlled, "you know that I care for you deeply. I've admired you for some time, and I've come to understand that my life would be much better with you as a part of it. Just look at that silky blond hair and those ocean deep eyes. I know you might get this often. Because look at you, any man would fall for you, but I am not any man, Amelia."

Amelia's heart sank as the familiar speech began. William had expressed his intentions more than once, and each time, she had found herself gently repelling his advances, always finding some reason to delay what she knew was unpreventable.

"I appreciate your kindness, Mr. Crawford," she said softly, "but I—"

"Please," he interrupted, his tone firmer now, "call me William. There's no need for formalities between us, not when I've made my feelings so clear."

She nodded, feeling the weight of his expectations pressing down on her chest. "William, you've been very nice to my father and me and we're forever grateful for all you've done. But…"

She trailed off, searching for the right words. How could she explain that her heart was no longer there to give? How could she tell him about the mysterious musician who had filled her thoughts since that first encounter in the chapel? And that there is no more left for a possessive want to be gentleman searching for a beauty to show off.

William leaned closer, his face softening as he took her hand. "I don't want to rush you, Amelia," he said, his voice gentle, "but I must be honest—I find myself thinking more and more about our future. I've already spoken with your father, and he agrees that a marriage between us would be beneficial. There should stand nothing between us and you will be forever happy with me."

Amelia's breath caught in her throat. She knew her father's bakery was struggling, and William's gifts had kept them afloat. The idea of securing their future should have been comforting, but instead, it felt like a trap.

But before she could respond, the bakery door swung open again, and a bunch of laughter and noise filled the room as a group of children ran in, chasing each other around the counter. The sudden noise broke the tension, and Amelia quickly pulled her hand away, very grateful for the distraction.

William straightened his expression as he stood up from his seat. "I'll take my leave for now," he said, his voice abrupt. "But I hope you'll consider what I've said. I only want what's best for you, Amelia."

She nodded, finding her unable to find the right words to respond. William gave her a lingering look before he turned and walked out, the door closing behind him with a soft thud.

As the sound of his footsteps faded away, Amelia let out a shaky breath. She knew she couldn't keep avoiding this forever. But as her thoughts drifted back to the mysterious musician, she realized that her heart was already leading her down a different path, one that might not align with the intentions of William Crawford.

For now, all she wanted do was follow where that melody was, even if it meant ignoring the expectations of those around her.

Chapter 3: The Man in the Chapel

As the sun climbed higher casting shadows across the village, Amelia grabbed a bag full of breads and pastries, told her dad she would be going out to the village, gave him a kiss on the cheek and ran off. Her heart raced with excitement as she made her way toward the old chapel at the edge of Rosemoor. The path ran through a bunch of trees, their leaves whispering secrets in the breeze. With each step, the weight of Williams's words faded away, replaced by the thrill of the unknown.

When she reached the chapel, she paused for a moment at the entrance, gathering her courage. As the ancient stone building stood before her, its weathered facade covered in creepy ivy. The door creaked as she gently pushed it open, revealing the worn-down interior.

Inside, the air was cool and still, dust particles dancing in the rays of light that filtered through the stained-glass windows. And there, sitting at the grand but neglected piano, was Edward Sinclair.

He didn't notice her at first because of his eyes being closed, as his fingers moved gracefully over the keys, playing a melody that seemed to fill the empty space with a downhearted beauty. The music was both haunting and comforting, as if it carried all her unspoken emotions of the past.

Amelia stood at the doorstep, captivated by the sight of him. Edward was playing in a quiet, unassuming way. His dark hair fell in loose waves over his forehead, and his face, youthful, bore the traces of sorrow and experience far beyond his years. He wore simple clothes, paint-stained—a complete contrast to William's polished wardrobe—but there was this depth to him that drew her to him, a mystery she felt wanting to be uncovered.

As the final notes of the piece faded into silence, Amelia took a hesitant step forward, her step echoing in the stillness. Edward's eyes snapped open, and he turned to face her, surprise flickering across his face.

"I'm sorry," she stumbled, suddenly self-conscious under his gaze. "I didn't mean to intrude. The music... it just drew me in."

For a moment, Edward said nothing, his eyes studying her with an intensity that made her heart skip a beat. Then, a small, almost shy smile curved his lips. "You're not intruding," he said softly. His voice was warm, with a slight accent that hinted at a life lived far off this quiet village. "I'm glad someone appreciates it. I wasn't sure if anyone even visited this place anymore."

Amelia returned his smile, relief overcoming her. "I come here sometimes, to think. It's so peaceful. And your music... it's beautiful. I've never heard anything like it."

Edward's expression softened at her words, and he made a small gesture to the bench beside him. "Would you like to sit?" he asked. "I was just about to play something else, if you'd care to listen."

Amelia hesitated only for a moment before walking across the room and taking a seat beside him. Up close, she could see the faint smudges of colour on his hands, the signs of an artist. There was a quiet intensity about him, a focus that seemed to follow along every step he made.

"Do you live in the village?" she asked, curious to know more about this charismatic stranger.

Edward shook his head. "No, I'm just passing through. I just needed a change of scenery... somewhere to clear my mind and find inspiration. I used to live in the city, but it became too much." His voice held a hint of bitterness, but it was quickly overcome by a practiced calm.

"And have you found what you're looking for?" asked Amelia curiously.

Edward paused, his gaze drifting to the piano keys. "In some ways, yes," he said, his tone thoughtful. "But in others, I'm still searching. Music helps. It's like a language of its own, one that speaks when your words fail."

Amelia nodded, understanding it too well. "I feel the same about this place," she confessed. "There's something about the chapel... it makes me feel like I can breathe here, like I can be myself and come out of my shell."

They sat in complete silence for a moment, the weight of their unspoken thoughts hanging between them. Then, with a sudden gesture, Edward began to play again, this time a softer, more hopeful tune. Amelia closed her eyes, letting the music wash over her, and in that moment, she felt a connection—a bond between them that went beyond words.

When the music finally came to an end, Edward looked at her, his eyes searching hers. "I don't know why," he said quietly, "but I feel like we were meant to meet. Like there's something, between us."

Amelia's breath caught in her throat. She knew she should be cautious, should protect her heart against the emotions storming inside her. But there was something about Edward—his honesty, his vulnerability—that made her want to take the risk.

"Maybe we were," she whispered, a small smile pulling at the corners of her lips. "Maybe this is where your search ends."

Edward's smile widened, and for the first time in a long while, Amelia felt a flicker of hope—a sense that perhaps, in this forgotten chapel at the edge of Rosemoor, she had found something important, something worth holding onto.

But as the shadows became longer and the day began to fade, a lingering doubt remained in the very back of her mind. She couldn't forget William, or the promises she had made to her father. Her path ahead was uncertain, and she knew that the choices she would soon have to make could change everything.

Yet, as she looked at Edward, she couldn't help but feel that, whatever happened, this was where she was meant to be.

Chapter 4: Whispers of the Heart

Over the next few weeks, Amelia found herself drawn back to the chapel again and again. Each visit with Edward was like discovering a new piece of herself, parts she hadn't even realized were missing. They spent hours talking about art, music, and life, their conversations flowing so natural like the river that flows through Willowbrook. With Edward, Amelia felt a freedom she had never felt neither known—a sense that she could be herself, unbothered by the expectations that waited so anxiously for her at home.

But even as her heart opened to this new, fragile happiness, a shadow loomed over her thoughts. William Crawford's visits to the bakery became more and more frequent, his intentions clearer with each passing day. Amelia could feel the pressure mounting up, like a grip tightening around her heart. She knew she couldn't keep her two worlds separate forever, and the thought of them colliding filled her with fear.

One evening, as the sun lowered below the horizon and the sky painted by the colours of nightfall, Amelia met Edward at the chapel once again. He was waiting for her inside, his back turned as he studied one of the stained-glass windows, its colours softened by the graceful light.

"Edward," she called softly, and he turned to face her, a smile brightening up his features.

"Amelia," he replied, crossing the room to meet her. He took her hands in his, his skin warm and making her feel safe. "I was beginning to think you wouldn't come."

"I almost didn't," she admitted, her voice tinted with the anxiety she had been trying to suppress all day. "There's so much I need to say... so much I don't know how to explain."

Edward's brow furrowed, concern flickering in his eyes. "What's wrong?" he asked, his tone gentle but insistent. "You can tell me anything, you know that."

She looked down at their holding hands, her heart aching with the weight of her emotions. "It's William," she began, the words catching in her throat. "He... he wants to marry me. And my father, he thinks it's a good match. William's done so much for us, and I—I don't know what to do."

Edward's grip tightened slightly, and when she looked up, she saw a storm brewing behind his calm exterior. "And what do you want, Amelia?" he asked, his voice steady but mixed with a tone she hadn't heard before. "Do you love him?"

The question hung in the air between them, heavy and unavoidable. Amelia shook her head, tears forming in her eyes. "No," she whispered, with a shaky voice. "I don't. I never have. But I don't know how to say no. My family is depending on him."

Edward's expression softened, and he wrapped his hand around her delicate face, his thumb wiping away the tears that had begun to fall. "Amelia," he said, his voice filled with a quiet intensity, "you deserve to be happy. You deserve to choose your own path, not to be forced into something that isn't right for you. I... I care about you. More than I've cared about anyone in a long time. And I can't stand by and watch you be trapped in a life that you don't want."

His words pierced through her like a knife, the sincerity and passion in his voice striking something deep within her. She knew he was right, but the fear of disappointing her father and the guilt of turning away from someone who had been so kind weighed so heavily on her.

"I don't want to lose you," she confessed, her voice barely more than a whisper. "But I don't know how to make this work. William won't take no for an answer, and I can't bear to hurt my father."

Edward was silent for a moment, his thumb gently stroking her cheek as he thought about her words. "Then let me help you," he said finally, his tone firm. "Let me talk to your father. I'll explain everything. He deserves to know how you really feel. And as for William... if he truly cares for you, he'll understand. And if he doesn't—" Edward paused, the fire in his eyes growing. "—then he doesn't deserve you."

Amelia's heart swelling at his words and a flicker of hope sparking in her. She could have never imagined that someone would fight for her, would stand by her side in this way. And yet here was the man of her dreams, offering her not just his support, but also his love.

But even as she nodded, agreeing to let him help, a part of her couldn't shake the fear that this wouldn't end as easily as Edward believed. William wasn't the type of man to give up what he wanted, but also her father—who had always been concerned with stability—might not understand her choice.

Still, as she looked into Edward's eyes, she knew she had to try. For the first time in her life, she wanted to fight for something. And with Edward by her side, she felt that maybe, just maybe, she could win.

Chapter 5: A Dangerous Game

The next day, as the sun cast a warm glow over the village, Edward followed Amelia to her home. The Hartley bakery was packed with its usual morning crowd, but as they approached, Amelia's anxiety grew. She had never disobeyed her father before, never stood against the expectations that had always been put on her.

When they entered the shop, her father looked up from the counter, his eyes lighting up at the sight of his daughter. But when he noticed Edward beside her, his smile faded, replaced by a look of curiosity with a hit of concern.

"Amelia," he greeted her, wiping his flour-covered hands on his apron. "Who's this you've brought with you?"

"This is Edward Sinclair," Amelia began, her voice stumbling slightly. "He's a... a friend."

Edward stepped forward, reaching his hand out. "It's a pleasure to meet you, Mr. Hartley. Amelia has spoken very highly of you."

Mr. Hartley took his hand, shaking it firmly. "A friend, eh?" he said, eyeing Edward with a mix of caution and interest. "Well, any friend of Amelia's is welcome here. What can I do for you?"

Amelia swallowed hard, her heart beating faster. "Father, there's something I need to talk to you about. It's... it's important."

Mr. Hartley's expression shifted, his brow moving up as he glanced from his daughter to Edward. "Alright," he said slowly, setting aside his gloves. "Let's talk. Come to the back, where we can have some privacy."

The three of them moved to the small kitchen at the back of the bakery, where the scent of freshly baked bread was mixed with the tension in the air. Mr. Hartley gestured for them to sit, then took a seat himself, his gaze fixed on Amelia.

"What's this about, Amelia?" he asked, his tone serious.

Amelia hesitated, glancing at Edward for reassurance. He gave her a small nod, urging her to speak. Taking a deep breath, she turned back to her father.

"It's about William Crawford," she began, her voice steady despite the storm inside her.

"He's been talking about marriage... about our future. But, Father, I don't love him. I don't want to marry him. I can't."

Mr. Hartley's eyes widened in surprise, and he sat back in his chair, absorbing her words. "But Amelia," he said after a moment, his tone puzzled, "William is a good man. He's been good to us. Why wouldn't you want to marry him? He could provide for you, give you a stable life. Isn't that what you want?"

Amelia shook her head, her heart pounding. "I want to be happy, Father. I want to choose my own path. William might be a good man, but he's not the man I love."

Mr. Hartley's gaze flicked to Edward, and understanding dawned in his eyes. "And what about this young man?" he asked, his tone cautious. "Is he the one you love?"

Amelia nodded, tears welling in her eyes. "Yes, Father. I've never felt this way before. Edward makes me feel alive, like I can be myself. I know it's not what you expected, but... I can't marry William."

Mr. Hartley was silent for a long moment, his expression unreadable. When he finally spoke, his voice was quiet, almost submissive. "Amelia, I just want what's best for you. I want you to be safe, to have a good life. If Edward is the one who makes you happy, then... then maybe that's what's best. But you have to consider, William won't take this lightly. He's not a man who's used to being told no."

Edward, who had been listening quietly, leaned forward. "Mr. Hartley," he said earnestly, "I know this might be difficult, but I promise you, I will take care of Amelia. I will do whatever it takes to make her happy. I understand the risks, and I'm willing to face them. But I can't do it without your blessing."

Mr. Hartley studied Edward carefully, his eyes searching the young man's face for any sign of uncertainty. Edward met his gaze steadily, his decision clear in every line of his expression.

"Edward," Mr. Hartley began, his voice measured, "I can see that you're sincere, and I can tell that you care deeply for my daughter. But you must understand the position I'm in. William has been a pillar of support for this family. He's helped us when no one else would, and he expects something in return."

Amelia's heart sank as her father spoke, the weight of her responsibility pressing down on her like a stone. She knew the truth of his words—William had indeed been generous to them, and in the small village of Rosemoor, refusing duties like these were not taken lightly.

"I know, Father," she whispered, her voice full with desperation. "But my heart... my heart belongs to Edward. I can't live a lie, not for anyone. Please, I'm begging you, don't make me do this."

Mr. Hartley sighed heavily; his wrinkly face carved with lines of worry. He looked at his daughter, his expression softening as he saw the fear and determination in her eyes. He knew how much this decision would cost her, how it would change the course of her life forever.

"Amelia," he said softly, reaching out to take her hand, "I want you to be happy. Truly, I do. But the world isn't always kind to those who follow their hearts. I've seen what happens to people who confront their expectations, who go against the duties. It's not easy, and it's not always fair."

He paused, glancing over at Edward, who was watching the exchange with a mixture of hope and unease. "But," Mr. Hartley continued, his voice firming, "if this is truly what you want, if Edward is the man you've chosen, then I won't stand in your way. I'll talk to William myself. It won't be easy, and it won't be pleasant, but I'll do it for you,

Amelia. Just... be sure this is the path you want to take."

Tears of happiness streamed down Amelia's cheeks as she threw her arms around her father, overcome with relief and gratitude. "Thank you, Father," she whispered, her voice overwhelmed with emotion. "Thank you for understanding."

Edward stood up, his own heart swelling with a mixture of joy and relief. He had prepared himself for the worst, for a refusal, but instead, he had been given a chance—a chance to build a life with the woman he loved.

Mr. Hartley rose slowly from his chair, his gaze now fixed on Edward. "You'd better take good care of her, young man," he said, his tone serious but not unkind. "Amelia is my only daughter, and she deserves the best."

Edward nodded formally. "I will, sir. You have my word."

But even as the words left his lips, a shadow of doubt crept into Edward's mind. He knew Wiliam Crawford wasn't the type to take rejections lightly. There would be consequences, of that he was certain. The road ahead of them was far from clear, and the risks were great.

As they left the bakery that evening, hand in hand, Amelia felt a strange mix of hope and fear. She had taken the first step toward claiming her own happiness, but deep down, she knew that this was just the beginning. The storm was coming, and when it hit, everything would change.

For now, though, she allowed herself to savour this moment of victory, this brief silence before the unavoidable storm with William Crawford. She looked up at Edward, her heart swelling up with love and gratefulness, and knew that no matter what lay ahead, she was not going to face it alone.

Chapter 6: Passion and Darkness

Every of Amelias days became a mix of joy and tension, each emotion fighting to take over her heart. The time that she spent with Edward was like something straight out of a dream—filled with whispered promises and secret smiles, moments that felt too romantic to be real. They met in the hidden corners of Rosemoor, in the shade of the old oak tree by the river or the quiet niches of the village's forgotten paths, far from hovering eyes.

In those stolen hours, the world seemed to consist of just the two of them. Edward would speak of the future, painting beautiful pictures with his words—of the life they could build together, where love, not duty, would be the foundation.

He shared his dreams of becoming an artist, of traveling to distant lands and cities to capture the beauty of the world on canvases. Amelia would listen, her heart swelling with the possibility of a life beyond the restraints of Rosemoor, a life where she could be more than just the daughter that had to fulfil her duty or an obedient wife.

One afternoon, as they lay beneath the old Oaktree, Edward turned to her, his expression serious. "Amelia," he began, taking her hand, "I want you to know that I'm serious about our future. I'll find a way to make it work, to give us a life together. I'll paint, I'll sell my work, I'll make money in anyway—we'll find a way, I promise."

Amelia looked into his eyes, seeing the honesty of his love and the determination that lay beneath those golden-hazel eyes. "I believe you, Edward," she whispered, her voice filled with emotion. "I know it won't be easy, but as long as we're together, I don't care about the rest."

They sealed their promises with a kiss, the world around them fading away as they lost themselves in each other. But even as their love spread in the light of the golden sun, a shadow loomed over their happiness, one that grew darker with each passing day.

William Crawford, once patient and composed, had begun to change. His demeanour, which was once warm and attentive, became cold and possessive. He would visit Amelia more frequently, as he seemed to be concerned for her well-being, but she could see that shift in his eyes—the way he watched her, as if she were something he owned rather than someone he cared for.

He began to include himself into her daily routine, arriving unannounced at the bakery or insisting on accompanying her on long walks through the village. What once felt like simple kindness now felt like a sling thrown around her neck tightening around it, with every gesture he reminded her of his control slowly consuming her life like a wave not being able to stop, and no matter how fast she ran it seemed to be able to catch up to her anyhow.

One evening, after another suffocating encounter with William, Amelia found herself at the riverside, her mind twirling with confusion and fear. Edward was already there, waiting for her with concern carved on his face.

"Amelia, what's wrong?" he asked, pulling her into his arms as she fell against him.

"It's William," she whispered, her voice barely noticeable. "He's changing, Edward. He's becoming... a possessive monster. He watches me all the time, he won't leave me alone. I feel like I'm losing control of my own life."

Edward's expression darkened, anger flashing through his eyes. "I've noticed it too," he said, his voice low. "He's not the man he pretends to be. He's trying to control you, Amelia, and I won't let him. We have to find a way out of this."

Amelia nodded, her heart pounding with fear. "But how? He's so powerful here, everyone looks up to him. And my father... he's so grateful to William for everything he's done for us. How can I go against that?"

Edward took her hands, his grip firm and reassuring. "We'll find a way," he said, his voice steady. "I won't let him take you from me. We'll talk to your father, we'll leave Rosemoor if we have to. But you don't have to face this alone, Amelia. I'm always by your side, and I'm not going anywhere."

Their bond grew stronger with each passing day. But so did the tension, as William's sling on Amelia's neck tightened even more. He began to make more pointed comments about their future together; about the life he expects them to build. That he would bring her gifts—jewels, fine dresses—things that should have filled her with joy, but it instead felt like chains being wrapped around her soul.

One evening, he presented her a particularly extravagant necklace. As William put it on, Amelia felt the weight of it like the sling around her neck once again. "It's beautiful, William," she said, forcing a smile, but inside she was petrified and sobbing.

"Only the best for my future wife," William replied, his tone smooth but his eyes cold. "You deserve even more, Amelia. Soon, we'll be married, and I can give you all the things you dream of. Everything will be perfect."

His words, once so harmless, now filled her with fear. She felt trapped, suffocated by the role she was being forced to play in her own life. But every time she thought of running, of escaping with Edward to some distant place, beyond the horizon where they could be free, leave all their sorrows and problems in the village, the reality of her situation crushed her hopes.

As the days followed on, the contrast between her time with Edward and her time with William became unbearable. With Edward, she was free—free to laugh, to dream, to be herself. But with William, she was only a shadow of who she once was, caught in a web of expectations and obligations she could never fulfil. He just saw her as a soulless case, a pretty puppet he could show off and control.

And so, the lovers continued their secret meetings, their love becoming deeper with time, even as they saw the intimidating clouds gathering at the horizon. They knew they had little time before they would have to make a choice—a choice that would decide their course of life.

But for now, they just clung to each other for as long as possible, finding comfort in the love that had formed despite all their problems, unaware of the trials that awaited them in the days to come.

Chapter 7: Unspoken Fears

The days in Rosemoor had grown shorter and the sun sinking earlier beneath the horizon with each evening. The once vibrant colours of autumn had started to fade, and the trees stood bare, their brittle branches reaching out for the darkening sky like skinny fingers. The chill in the air resembled the tension that had settled over Amelia's heart, a tension that seemed to thicken with every encounter with William Crawford.

Amelia's time with Edward had become the highlight of her day, a brief escape from the pressures of her daily life. Their love had flourished in secret, growing stronger with every whispered promise and shared dream. But the outside world was closing in on them, and this safe feeling they had found in each other's arms was beginning to feel vulnerable.

One evening, as the last light of the day cast long shadows across the fields, Amelia and Edward met at their usual spot by the river. The air was heavy with the scent of wet earth and fallen leaves, the quiet whispers of the water providing a soothing backdrop to their conversation. Yet despite the peaceful surroundings, Amelia's heart was anything but calm.

"Edward," she began, her voice sprinkled with worry, "I don't know how much longer we can keep this up. William is growing more suspicious by the day. I'm afraid of what might happen if he finds out about us."

Edward took her hand in his, his touch calming her as it always did. "I know, Amelia. I've noticed the way he looks at you, the way he watches you when you're not looking. It's as if he's waiting for you to slip, to give him a reason to confront you."

Amelia shuddered at the thought, her mind racing with the possibilities. "I hate this feeling of being trapped, of having to live in secret. I wish things were different. I wish we could just be together without all these complications."

Edward's eyes softened with sympathy. "I wish that too, more than anything. But we have to be careful, Amelia. I don't want to see you hurt, and I don't want to be the cause of any more trouble for you or your family."

Amelia nodded; her throat filled with emotion. "I know. But I can't help feeling like it's all closing in on me, like I'm being suffocated by the expectations and burden that everyone has placed on me."

Edward was about to respond when the sound of rustling leaves reached their ears. They both turned, and Amelia's heart skipped a beat as William Crawford emerged from the trees, his expression dark and foreboding.

"So," William began, his voice low and cold, "this is where you've been sneaking off to, Amelia."

Amelia's breath caught in her throat, her pulse quickening with fear. "William... I—"

"Save your excuses," William interrupted, his gaze shifting to Edward with barely concealed disgust. "I should have known. You've been lying to me, to your family, to everyone. What were you planning to do, Amelia? Run off with this... painter?"

Edward's hand tightened around Amelia's, his protective instincts kicking in. "William, calm down. We were—"

"You were what?" William snapped, stepping closer. "Sneaking around behind my back? Making a fool of me in front of the entire town?"

Amelia could feel the ground slipping away beneath her feet, the fragile peace she had tried to maintain shattering before her eyes. "William, please listen—"

"No, Amelia," William cut her off, his voice shaking with hardly suppressed rage. "You listen. Do you have any idea what you're risking? What this will do to your father's reputation? To his business? He's already struggling to keep the bakery afloat, and now you're throwing everything away for some foolish affair?"

Amelia felt tears welling in her eyes, her heart breaking at the harshness in William's words. "It's not like that, William. I care about Edward, I really do. But I never meant to hurt anyone."

William's eyes narrowed, his gaze switching between her and Edward. "You didn't mean to hurt anyone? Amelia, you're playing with fire, and it's not just you who's going to get burned. Think about your father. Think about your family. They depend on you, and you're willing to throw it all away for a man who can't even provide for you?"

Edward stiffened at the accusation, but he kept his voice calm. "I may not have wealth, William, but I can offer Amelia something that money can't buy. I can offer her love, respect, and the freedom to be herself. Isn't that worth more than all the materialistic things you can provide?"

William's face twisted with anger. "Love? Respect? Those are nothing but empty words if you can't back them up with action. Do you think love will keep a roof over her head? Will respect put food on the table?

You're living in a fantasy, Sinclair. And you're dragging Amelia down with you."

Amelia's heart ached at his rough words. She knew he was trying to protect her, but his possessiveness and control were suffocating. She had never felt so torn, so lost between two worlds—one of security and duty, the other of passion and freedom.

Edward's voice was firm as he addressed William. "Amelia deserves to make her own choices, to decide what's best for her. She's not a prize to be won or a possession to be controlled."

William's eyes flashed with fury. "And you think you're the one who knows what's best for her? You, who can barely survive by himself? You have no idea what it takes to build a life, to care for a family. You're nothing but a dreamer, and you're leading her into a nightmare."

Amelia's tears spilled over, her emotions threatening to overwhelm her. "Please, stop," she begged, her voice trembling. "This isn't helping. You're both tearing me apart, and I don't know what to do."

William's expression softened slightly at the sight of her tears, but his resolve remained firm. "Amelia, you need to think about what you're doing. If you continue down this path, there will be consequences. Not just for you, but for everyone you care about."

The weight of his words settled heavily on Amelia's chest. She could feel the pressure mounting, the expectations of her family, her community, and even William himself pressing in on her from all sides. The future she had once dreamed of with Edward now seemed like a distant fantasy, overshadowed by the harsh reality of her situation.

Edward, seeing the turmoil in Amelia's eyes, stepped closer, his voice filled with gentle reassurance. "Amelia, I know this is a hard time for all of us. But whatever happens, I'll be here for you. I love you, and I want you to be happy, even if that means letting you go."

But even as he spoke, Amelia knew that the decision before her was not one that could be made easily. The love she felt for Edward was real, deep, and undeniable, but so too was the duty she had to fulfil for her family and the life she had always known.

William, sensing her hesitation, pressed his advantage. "Amelia, this isn't just about you and Edward. It's about your father, your family's future. You can't afford to be selfish now."

The word "selfish" cut through Amelia like a knife. She had always tried to do what was right, to put others before herself, but now she was being asked to sacrifice the one thing she had ever truly wanted for herself — her happiness with Edward.

The silence that followed was heavy, each passing moment filled with unspoken words and mounting tension. Amelia's mind raced, her heart aching with the weight of the choice she knew she would have to make.

But that choice would not come tonight.

As the evening darkened into night, William finally broke the silence, his voice calm and steady, "We'll discuss this later, Amelia. For now, I suggest you think long and hard about what you want and what you're willing to give up."

With that, William turned on his heel and walked away, leaving Amelia and Edward standing alone in the growing darkness. The river's gentle rushing melody was the only sound that broke the stillness, but it did little to calm the storm raging in Amelia's heart.

Edward watched William's retreating figure, his jaw clenched with frustration and worry. He turned to Amelia, his eyes filled with concern. "Are you alright?"

Amelia nodded, but the gesture was half-hearted. "I don't know, Edward. I don't know what to do."

Edward reached out and pulled her into his arms, holding her close as the tears she had been holding back broke free again. "We'll figure it out," he mumbled, his voice soft and comforting. "We'll find a way, Amelia. I promise."

But even as he held her, Amelia couldn't shake the feeling that the walls were closing in, that the life she had dreamed of with Edward was slipping further and further out of reach.

The night air was cold against her skin, and for the first time, Amelia felt truly afraid—not just of what lay ahead, but of what she might lose in the process.

Chapter 8: The Weight of Expectations

The cold air of winter began to settle down in Rosemoor, the once vibrant village was now covered in a layer of frost. The days were short and grey, the nights long and bitter. But the coldest chill of all was the one that had settled over Amelia's heart.

Since the night of the confrontation by the river, Amelia had felt the weight of the world pressing down on her shoulders. Her father's quiet disappointment, the knowing glances from the townsfolk, and the consistent presence of William Crawford all there as constant reminders of the impossible choice she had to make.

Her father, Mr. Hartley, had always been a man of few words, but in the weeks that followed, his silence became deeper than ever before, almost unbearable. The once warm and comforting atmosphere of their home had turned tense and heavy, the unspoken expectations suffocating Amelia with everyday going by.

"Amelia," her father began one evening as they sat by the fire, with the only sound in the room being the crackling sound of the burning logs. "William came by today."

Amelia's heart sank, her hands shaking slightly as she set aside her sewing. "Oh?"

Mr. Hartley nodded; his expression unreadable. "He's concerned about you. He says you've been distant, that you're not yourself."

Amelia looked down at her hands, unable to look at her father. "I'm just... tired, Father. It's been a lot to process."

Her father sighed deeply, leaning back in his chair. "Amelia, I know this is difficult for you. But William is a good man. He cares for you, and he can provide you with a stable life. That's everything a father could want for his daughter."

Amelia bit her lip, the familiar ache in her chest returning. "But Father, what if that's not what I want? What if... what if I don't love him?"

Mr. Hartley's eyes softened, but his voice remained firm. "Love is important, Amelia, but so is security. Life isn't always about what we want. Sometimes, it's about doing what's right, what's necessary. You have a duty to this family, to the life we've built here. I can't protect you forever, and

William... he's willing to take on that responsibility."

The words pierced deep into her heart, a strong reminder of the expectations that had been placed on her from the moment she was born. Amelia's life had always been just about duty—duty to her family, to her community, to the legacy her father had worked so hard to maintain. But now, that duty felt like a prison.

In the days that followed, the pressure only intensified. The women in the village, who had once greeted her with warm smiles, now looked at her with a mixture of pity and judgment. The whispers that followed her as she walked through the market were like knives in her back, each one a reminder of the scandal that was brewing beneath the surface and waiting to overflow.

"Have you heard? Amelia Hartley still hasn't given William an answer."

"Such a shame. Her poor father must be beside himself."

"She's a good girl, but it's time she faced reality. William is the best option she has."

At home, it wasn't any better, her father's quiet insistence was becoming harder to bear. He would mention William's name more often, speak of the future with a certainty that left hardly any room for Amelia's own hopes and dreams. She felt trapped, caught between the life she had always known and the love she had found with Edward, a love that now seemed like a distant memory.

The tension was beginning to take a visible grip on her. Her once bright eyes had dulled, dark circles forming beneath them from nights spent tossing and turning, her mind racing with worry and doubt. Her appetite had faded, and she found herself growing weaker, the weight of her burden being too much for her to carry alone.

Edward noticed the change in her, his concern growing daily. Whenever they managed to steal a moment together, he would gently take her hands in his and ask, "Amelia, what's wrong? You don't look well."

Amelia would force a smile, trying to reassure him, but the effort only seemed to drain her further. "I'm just tired, Edward," she would say, even though they both knew there was more than that. The love they shared had become a source of both strength and sorrow, a flickering light in a world growing darker around them.

One afternoon, after a particularly exhausting day, Amelia found herself alone in her room, staring out the window at the snow-covered fields beyond. The beauty of the winter landscape was lost on her; all she could feel was the frost leaking into her bones, a chill that seemed to drain her life out of her. She hadn't felt truly warm in weeks.

As she sat there, her thoughts spiralling into sorrows, when there was a knock at the door. Before she could respond, her father entered, his expression serious.

"Amelia," he said quietly, closing the door behind him. "We need to talk."

She turned to face him, fear forming in her stomach. "What is it, Father?"

He sighed, sitting down beside her on the bed. For a long moment, he simply looked at her, his eyes filled with a mix of concern and something else.

"Amelia," he began, his voice softer than usual, "I've been thinking a lot about what's been happening... about you and William. I know this isn't easy for you, but you have to understand the position we're in. Our family... we're not as secure as we once were. The bakery has been struggling, and if things don't soon improve, I'm not sure how much longer we can hold ourselves afloat."

Amelia's heart sank. She had known the bakery was facing difficulties, but hearing her father speak of it so plainly made the situation so real. "Father, I didn't realize it was that bad..."

Mr. Hartley nodded; his expression worried. "It is. And William... he's offered to help. He's willing to invest in the bakery, to keep it afloat. But there's a condition, Amelia. He wants to know what you think. He wants to know if you'll be his wife."

The words hung heavy in the air, each one landing like an arrow to Amelia's already fragile spirit. She felt as the air was getting heavier, the room growing smaller and more suffocating with each passing second.

"Father," she whispered, her voice trembling, "this isn't fair. I can't—"

"I know, Amelia," her father interrupted gently, placing a hand on her arm. "I know this isn't what you want to hear. But we don't always get to choose our path.

Sometimes, the choices are made for us. Sometimes life isn't fair. I don't want to see you suffer, but I also don't want to see our family lose everything we've worked so hard for and also you lose the life you've known."

As tears were forming in Amelia's eyes, she looked at her father, the man who had always been her rock, her protector. Now, he was asking her to sacrifice the one thing she had ever wanted for herself—for the sake of their family, for the sake of survival.

"I'm not asking you to make a decision right now," Mr. Hartley continued, his voice heavy with emotion. "But you need to think about it, Amelia. Think about what's at stake."

With that, he rose from the bed and left the room, leaving Amelia alone with her thoughts.

As the days passed, the pressure from the community grew even more. Everywhere Amelia went, she could feel the eyes of the townsfolk on her, their whispers and knowing looks following her like shadows. She was no longer just Amelia Hartley; she had become the prime subject of the village's gossip, the girl who couldn't make up her mind.

Her health continued to decrease, the constant stress and anxiety tearing her apart. She could barely eat, could barely sleep, her dreams haunted by visions of a future she couldn't escape. Even her once cherished moments with Edward had become tinged with sadness, the love they shared overshadowed by the looming threat of what was to come.

Edward, grew more and more concerned. "Amelia," he would say, his voice filled with worry, "this can't go on. You're not well. Please, let me help you."

But what could he do? Amelia knew that Edward's love was true, but it couldn't save her from the reality she faced. Her life was falling apart, and she felt as if she was being

slowly crushed beneath the weight of her obligations, her dreams slipping further and
further away.

And so, Amelia found herself standing at
the edge of an abyss, the ground crumbling
away beneath her feet. She knew that soon,
she would have to make a choice—a choice
that would determine not just her own future, but the future of her family, and of the
man she loved.

But now, she could only wait, her heart
heavy with fear and uncertainty, as the cold
winter days dragged on, each one bringing
her closer to the unavoidable.

Chapter 9: The Price of Love

The monotone chill of winter had by now completely surrounded the village, but it was nothing compared to the cold that had settled in Amelia's heart. The weight of the decision that she had to make was unbearable. She knew that the time for a decision had come, and with it, the end of the dreams she had once cherished.

For days, Amelia had wrestled with the impossible choice: to follow her heart with Edward or to secure her family's future with William. She could feel the eyes of the village on her, the whispers growing louder as the days passed, but it was rather the quiet desperation in her father's eyes that haunted her the most. He had given her time, but that time had run out by now.

One evening, after a once again long and sleepless night, Amelia found herself standing before the mirror in her room, staring at the reflection of a girl she barely recognized anymore. Her face was pale, her eyes hollow, and her hands trembled as they glid over the front of her dress. This was not the Amelia she had once been—carefree, full of life, and brimming with hope. That girl had been buried under expectations and lost to duty. In her place stood someone who was about to make a choice that would change her life forever.

With a deep breath, she made her way downstairs, her pulse increasing with every step. When she reached the living room, she found her father seated by the fire, the room warm but the atmosphere so ice cold. He looked up as she entered, his expression a mix of concern and quiet resignation.

"Amelia," he said softly, his voice filled with a gravity that made her heart ache. "Have you... have you made a decision?"

She nodded; her throat tight as she struggled to find the words. "Yes, Father. I have."

Mr. Hartley's eyes searched her face, seeing the pain carved there. "And?"

"I've decided to marry... William," she said, her voice barely more than a whisper. The words felt like shards of glass in her mouth, each one cutting deeper than the last.

For a moment, her father said nothing, only nodding slowly as he absorbed the weight of her decision. "You're doing the right thing, Amelia," he said finally, though his voice was tinged with sadness. "It's not an easy choice, but it's the one that will secure our future."

Amelia forced herself to a small, bitter smile. "Yes, Father. It's the right thing."

But as the words left her lips, she felt a part of herself die—a part that had once believed in love, in happiness, in a future that was hers to be shaped. That future was gone now, replaced by the cold reality of obligation.

The days that followed were a blur of wedding preparations and visits from William, who, seemed pleased with her decision, even though he could sense the sadness that lingered in her eyes. He was kind, even tender, in his own way of course, but there was a distance between them that could not be connected by words or gestures.

And then there was Edward.

She had avoided him since making her decision, unable to bear the thought of seeing the hurt in his eyes, the betrayal she knew he would feel. But Edward was not the type to simply fade into the background. One day, he came to see her, his face pale and his eyes searching as he found her alone in the garden, where she had gone to escape the uncomfortable atmosphere of the house.

"Amelia." he called softly as he approached, his voice filled with a mix of hope and fear.

She turned to face him, and the look in his eyes nearly shattered her. "Edward," she whispered, her heart breaking all over again.

"Is it true?" he asked, his voice trembling. "Are you really going to marry him?"

Amelia looked away, not being able to meet his gaze. "Yes," she said, the word heavy with finality.

Edward stared at her, his expression one of shock and disbelief. "But... why? I thought-" He stopped himself, shaking his head as if trying to clear the fog of confusion that had settled over him. "I thought you loved me,

Amelia. I thought we were going to be to-gether."

Tears welled in her eyes, and she blinked them back, forcing herself to stay strong. "I do love you, Edward. But this... this is bigger than us. My family... they need me to do this. I can't let them down. I can't be selfish."

"Selfish?" Edward's voice cracked with emotion. "Loving someone isn't selfish, Amelia. Wanting to be with the person you love isn't selfish. It's—" He stopped, his hands clenching into fists at his sides. "It's not fair."

"I know it's not fair." Amelia whispered, her voice breaking. "But it's the choice I have to make."

Edward's shoulders slumped, the fighting spirit draining out of him as he realized there was nothing more to say. "So that's it, then? You're choosing him over me?"

Amelia's heart ached with the pain of what she was about to say, but she knew it had to be said. "No," she said, her voice barely audible. "I'm choosing my family, over you."

For a long moment, Edward said nothing. He just looked at her, his eyes filled with a sorrow so deep, it threatened to drown them both. Then, without another word, he turned and walked away, with a silent tear on his cheek, leaving Amelia standing alone in the garden, the stillness around her deafening.

That evening, as the sun disappeared below the horizon, casting the world in a pink glow, Edward packed his belongings and left Rosemoor. He did not say goodbye to anyone, not even to Amelia. He simply disappeared, his heart shattered and his spirit broken, leaving behind the only life he had ever loved.

Amelia watched him leave from the window of her room, tears streaming down her face as she pressed her hand to the glass, as if to reach out to him one last time. But it was too late. Edward was gone, and with him went the last remnants of the future she had once dreamed so determent of.

The next morning, the village awoke to find Edward's small cottage abandoned, the door left wide open as if he had left in a hurry. The news spread quickly, and by midday, everyone in Rosemoor knew that Edward had gone. The whispers grew louder, but this time, they were tinged with sympathy, even the most judgmental among them could see the tragedy in what had happened.

Amelia, now more alone than ever, felt the full weight of her decision. She had chosen her family, her duty, her obligations—but in doing so, she had lost the one person who had ever truly understood her, who had loved her for who she was, not for what she could give.

And so, with a heart so heavy with sorrow, she could barely stand, Amelia began the long and painful process of preparing for a future she had never wanted, with a man she did not love. The winter grew colder, the days shorter, and Amelia could only hope that, in time, the pain would fade, that she would find some kind of peace in the life she had chosen.

But deep down, she knew that a part of her would always be missing, the part that had belonged to Edward—the part that would never, ever be there again.

Chapter 10: Fading Echoes

The day of Amelia's wedding to William was as grand as the town had already expected. The church was filled with flowers, the air filled with the scent of lilies and roses and a hint of sorrow, the seats were packed with villagers, eager to witness the union of two prominent families. Amelia stood at the altar, her hands clasped tightly around a bouquet, her white gown shimmering in the soft light.

But despite the beauty of the day, from then on, a cold emptiness settled in Amelia's heart.

As the wedding promises were spoken, her voice trembled. The words felt foreign on her tongue, hollow and meaningless. She glanced at William, standing tall and proud beside her. His smile was confident, almost triumphant, but there was no warmth in his eyes—only the satisfaction of winning.

She repeated after the priest, each phrase a weight on her soul: *to love, and to cherish...till death do us apart.* Her mind, however, wandered to Edward—his face, his touch, the way he had once made her feel alive. For a short moment, she imagined what it would have been like to stand here with him, to marry for love instead of duty. But that was not the reality.

The cheers erupted as the ceremony finished, the villagers celebrating the union of Amelia and William as if it were the perfect match. But as the bells rang, each ring echoed like a celebration to her inner death, in Amelia's mind. She forced a smile, accepting congratulations, and pretending for a moment that she was happy.

The reception that followed was lavish, filled with laughter, dancing, and the clinking of glasses. Amelia moved through the evening in a blur, making polite conversations and smiling grateful smiles, while her heart mourned the life she had let slip away.

That night, as she lay in the marital bed beside William, she stared at the ceiling, feeling more alone than she had ever been. The house was quiet, the festivities long over, and with each breath, the weight of her decision becoming reality. She had made her choice—for her family, for their security—

but it had cost her something she could never regain.

The years blurred together after that. Days turned into months, and months into years, marked by the changing of seasons and the quiet rhythm of the married life. The Amelia who had once dreamed of passion and happiness had disappeared, replaced by a dutiful wife who went through the actions of her role.

She performed her responsibilities with grace, attending to the house, hosting dinners, and managing the social circles of their village. Her father's bakery had grown successful, thanks to William's status, and her family was financially secure. By all means, her life seemed to have been perfect.

But behind closed doors, Amelia was crumbling.

As the seasons passed, the distance between her and William grew. He had never been cruel, but his possessiveness and control became more visible. They spoke of their future, their status, their wealth and the life they had built together, but never of love. He saw her more as an extension of his success, a prize that completed his image of the community.

For Amelia, every day felt like a slow suffocation. The house, large and grand, felt more like an extravagant cage, the rooms cold and empty. She had hoped that time might soften her heart toward William, that perhaps she might grow to care for him in some way, but that never happened, rather the opposite. Her love for Edward—though it had become a painful, distant memory—remained etched into her soul.

There were moments when she allowed herself to remember. In the silence of the early morning, when William was away on business, she would sit by the window, gazing out at the horizon. Her mind would drift back to those stolen moments with

Edward—his laughter, his touch, the way he had looked at her as if she were his entire world. In those brief moments, she felt it gave her strength again, even if only in memory.

But those memories, even though cherished, were bittersweet. They only served to remind her of what she had lost, of the life she could never have.

The weight of her regret began to manifest physically. Her once-vibrant health started to fade. At first, it was small things—headaches that lingered longer than they should, exhaustion that she couldn't seem to shake. But soon, it became clear that something was deeply wrong. She grew paler, her movements slower, and the fire in her eyes faded.

William, ever absorbed in his business and public image, noticed little. He provided for her in every material way, ensuring she had all the comforts and luxuries money could buy, but he could not give her the one thing she truly needed—caring. He never asked about her sadness, never questioned her declining health, as though he could not see the cracks in the woman he had married.

And Amelia, for her part, didn't tell him. She had chosen this life, and now, she had to live with the consequences.

By the time the fifth year of her marriage had passed, the once curious and loving Amelia, had now turned into an empty, lifeless body. She became a complete shadow of the woman she once was. Her days were spent in loneliness, wandering the halls of the house or resting in bed, the parts that were left of her body slowly giving in to the sorrow that had been eating away at her for years. The villagers, once so fascinated by her marriage, now whispered about her behind closed doors, wondering what had become of the once-bright Amelia Hartley.

Her father, too, had noticed the change. He visited often, his brow wrinkled with concern, but Amelia assured him she was fine. She couldn't bring herself to tell him the truth—that the life he had wanted for her had drained her of everything she had once been.

Still, every time she saw him, she smiled weakly and told him not to worry. After all, this was the life she had chosen. She had done her duty, secured her family's future, and now she was paying the price for it.

Chapter 11: Two Hearts so Empty

The years that separated Edward from Amelia passed like the pages of a forgotten book—torn, chaotic, and incomplete. After leaving the village, Edward had wandered, not knowing where to go or what to do. The pain of Amelia's choice still burned in his chest, raw and unforgiving, like an open wound that refused to heal.

But time, as it does, pushed him forward.

He wandered through cities far from the sleepy village where he had once dreamed of a future with her. In the aftermath of his heartbreak, grief consumed him, feasting on him from the inside out. With nowhere to place his sorrow, he turned to canvas—not out of his own will, but necessity. He painted blindly, pouring his pain, his memories, his unspoken words into colours and shapes. One canvas after another- witness to his pain, each brushstroke driven not by skill, but by feeling. What began as a desperate release slowly revealed something deeper. The rawness of his work, unfiltered and instinctive, began to draw attention. Melancholic scenes of grey depressing landscapes, deserted beaches, and rain-soaked streets spoke to something unspoken in others. There was a quiet and yet torturing sadness in his paintings, a depth of longing that related with anyone who had ever known the ache of such a lost love.

Edward became successful, though this meant little to him. Art collectors, galleries, and by walkers praised his work, calling him a visionary. He travelled from city to city, his paintings gaining popularity across the country, and yet with every new place, every new exhibition, his heart remained chained to the past—dominated by the memory of a woman he could never forget.

It was Amelia who lived in every brushstroke, her face in every shadow, her essence in every landscape. No matter how many years passed, no matter how far he travelled, she haunted him, her image for-ever imprinted on his soul.

On Amelia's side, who still remained in the tiny, monotone village of Rosemoor. The years since their last goodbye, Amelia's life had settled into a rhythm of predictability. Married to William, she played the role of the perfect wife—at least in public. She smiled at the right moments, attended the social gatherings she was required to go to, and performed her duties with efficiency. To the outside world, her life with William seemed one of stability and even success.

But inside the walls of their grand house, everything felt cold and lifeless.

William, though not overtly cruel, was distant, more focused on his business and the outward appearance of their life together than any real connection with Amelia. Their conversations were short, way too formal, revolving around the household or the village. He expected order, and Amelia provided it, maintaining the home with a quiet resignation. But there was no warmth between them, no laughter, no intimacy. It was as if she existed in a role—an actor in a play with no final act.

The coldness of their life together echoed in the way William would lay his hand on her shoulder briefly, like a reminder of ownership, not affection. His gaze never lingered on her, as if Amelia were no more than part of the house—an essential, yet unremarkable piece of his life.

And so, Amelia lived in silence.

But there were moments—small, brief moments—when Edward's memory slipped through the cracks in her carefully constructed façade.

In the evenings, after William had left for business or retired to his study, Amelia would retreat to her room. There, hidden in the bottom drawer of her dresser, was a small velvet box. She kept it hidden, tucked away beneath her layers of clothing, a secret she never dared to reveal to anyone. Inside the box lay the necklace Edward had given her on one of their stolen afternoons together—a simple, delicate piece with a silver pendant shaped like a rose.

It was her one link to him, the only physical reminder of the love they had shared.

On those quiet nights, when her choices felt unbearable, Amelia would open the box and let the cool metal of the necklace to rest in her palm. The touch of it brought back memories she tried so hard to suppress — Edward's smile, the way he had looked at her with such passion, the warmth of his hand as it closed around hers.

She would hold the necklace tightly, her heart aching with the knowledge of what could have been. She imagined, sometimes, that she could feel his presence, as if he were there with her, sitting in the silence, sharing the grief she could never say aloud.

These moments were always brief. The demands of her life with William would pull her back, and she would carefully place the necklace back in its box, close the drawer, and return to the life she had chosen. But the emptiness grew heavier with each passing year, and the memories of Edward only deepened the void within her.

Far away, in grand cities filled with busy streets and crowded galleries, Edward continued to paint. He found satisfaction in his work, though not the peace he so desperately wanted. Each canvas was a reflection of the inner landscape he could not escape—a place where time stood still, where shadows of the past stretched endlessly into the horizon.

He painted scenes that felt familiar, though they were always just a bit out of reach. Storms rolling over cliffs, waves crashing against empty shores, dark forests illuminated by fleeing rays of light—each painting spoke of a world suspended between hope and despair, a place where love had been lost and never recovered.

But one subject returned to him again and again: Amelia.

He never painted her directly. Instead, she lived in the details—the lone figure standing by the edge of a river, her back turned to the viewer; the hint of a woman's silhouette gazing out at the sea, her face hidden by mist. These were not portraits of her, but echoes — faint, fragmented reflections of the woman he had loved and lost.

Edward's success grew, and with it, the comments of critics and art lovers. But no matter how much praise he received, it meant nothing to him. He painted because it was the only way he could survive, the only way to release the pain that clung to him like a second skin.

Yet, with every stroke of the brush, he felt Amelia's absence more.

The world saw a brilliant artist, but Edward knew the truth. His heart had been left behind in that small village, with a woman who had chosen duty over love. No amount of success, no wealth or recognition, could fill the space she had left in his soul.

Amelia, too, continued to wither, her health declining slowly, almost unnotably.

The coldness of her marriage, the suffocating weight of her decision, was taking its consequences. She rarely left the house now, avoiding the social engagements that had once filled her calendar. Her body, much like her spirit, was slowly giving in.

Still, the necklace remained hidden in her drawer, untouched for long periods of time. But its presence, even unseen, was a reminder of the love she had lost—and the life she had chosen to endure.

Both she and Edward were trapped in their separate worlds, bound by a past they could never reclaim, and the love that had once been their strength and holding point had now become the source of their deepest sorrow.

Chapter 12: The Memory that Never Faded

The six years that have passed by now, had completely drained Amelia of her spirit, and now, as her illness took hold with a tight grip, she spent more and more time bounded to her room. The house that once seemed grand and full of promise now felt like a prison—a cage in which she had surrendered her freedom in exchange for a life of comfort, a decision she could no longer approve of.

Her illness had begun as a faint weakness, a persistent tiredness she couldn't shake, but it quickly progressed. The doctors spoke in vague terms—nothing could be done.

William, while attentive in arranging medical care, had become increasingly distracted by his business dealings. His visits to Amelia's bedside were brief, his conversations automatic. He asked if she needed anything but never cared long enough to hear her answer.

She was alone, both in her illness and in her heart.

The life she had once imagined—one filled with love, passion, and joy—had never materialized. Instead, she had lived a life of duty, of obligation, of quiet suffocation. And now, as the hours of her life decreased, the enormity of her regrets weighed heavily on her fragile body.

Amelia's thoughts turned often to Edward. Despite the years that had passed, his face remained vivid in her memory. She could still picture him—his smile, his eyes, the way he had looked at her with such tenderness and love. She had tried to forget him, tried to bury her feelings beneath her responsibilities, but he had never truly left her.

On one particularly quiet afternoon, the house safe from the distant ticking of the grandfather clock, Amelia found herself alone with her thoughts, her body weak and her mind drifting. William had not visited her that day. He had been away on business for weeks, and even when he was home, his presence was a distant one. The few words he exchanged with her were formal, detached, like speaking to a business partner rather than a wife. In his absence, Amelia had come to realize how little connection there had ever been between them.

Their marriage had been built on practicality, not love.

The cold, mechanical existence she had endured for so many years was now unravelling before her eyes. She thought of all the times she had stood by William's side, attending dinners, hosting guests, playing the role of the dutiful wife. But she had always felt a void within her, a longing for something that was missing—for someone, that was missing.

For Edward.

As the light from the window cast a soft glow over her pale porcelain skin, Amelia's gaze turned toward the drawer beside her bed. With a shaky hand, she reached for it, pulling it opens slowly. Inside, tucked away beneath papers and letters long forgotten, was the small velvet box that held the necklace Edward had given her all those years ago. She hadn't opened it in so long, afraid of the flood of memories it would bring, but now, in these final days, she could no longer resist.

Amelia opened the box and lifted the delicate silver pendant from its resting place. Feeling a rush of relief, yet also grief entering her body, just enough emotion to make her feel human again. It was cool against her skin, the rose-shaped charm shimmering in the fading sunlight. She held it in her hands, her fingers tracing its familiar silhouette. The feel of it brought back hundreds of memories—Edward's laughter, the way he had held her, the promises they had whispered to one another beneath the shade of the old oak tree.

Tears welled in her eyes, blurring her vision. She had tried so hard to be the woman her father wanted her to be, the woman society expected her to be. But in doing so, she had lost herself. And now, as her life neared its end, all she could think about was the life she could have had — the life she should have had — with Edward.

Her breath came in short, shallow gasps now, and the effort to hold the necklace felt overwhelming, yet she could not let go. She clutched it to her chest, the weight of her regrets pressing down on her. Her body ached, but it was the ache in her heart that consumed her.

"Edward..." she whispered, her voice barely audible, her lips trembling as she spoke his name.

It was the first time she had allowed herself to say it in years. The sound of it felt foreign, but at the same time, it filled her with a deep, aching sadness. She had loved him with all her heart, and yet she had let him go. For what? For security? For a life that had given her everything except the one thing she had truly wanted — love.

"Edward..." she whispered again, her voice breaking as tears slid down her cheeks. She closed her eyes, the weight of the pendant still resting against her chest, and for a moment, she allowed herself to imagine what might have been.

In her mind, she saw Edward's face, clear and vibrant, as though he were standing before her. She saw the life they might have shared—the love they might have nurtured together. She saw their walks through the fields, their laughter echoing in the air, their dreams unfolding before them. It was the life she had always dreamed of, the life that had slipped through her fingers.

The room around her grew dim, the world blurring at the edges as her strength faded. Her breaths were slow, but her mind was clear—clearer than it had been in years. She could feel herself slipping away, but it didn't frighten her anymore. In these final moments, she was at peace, not because she fulfilled her duty, but because in her heart, she was with Edward again.

Her fingers tightened around the necklace one last time, holding it close to her heart as her body grew still. The name of the man she had loved—and lost—was the last word on her lips.

"Edward..."

With that, Amelia's eyes peacefully closed, and the last remnants of her life faded away. Her heart, though broken, found a strange comfort in those final moments, consumed by the love that had remained within her, undying, until the very end.

Chapter 13: A Farewell Unspoken

The crisp morning air in Rosemoor felt different than Edward remembered. As his carriage rattled along the familiar, winding roads, the trees that lined the path seemed taller, more imposing, their branches casting long shadows over the ground. The fields, once golden with the warmth of summer, now lay buried under a grey sky. Everything had changed, and yet, in the deepest corners of his heart, nothing had changed at all.

He had never thought he would return to this place. Not after the way he had left, heartbroken and defeated. But the news had reached him only days ago — Amelia was ill, her health failing, her time running short. The moment he'd heard, his entire world had broken in two. He had to see her.

One last time.

The years had been kind to Edward in some way. His art had succeeded, and he had become a painter, his name celebrated in cities where ever he went. But no amount of success had ever filled the void Amelia had left behind. His paintings, though admired for their beauty, were sprinkled with sadness — each brushstroke haunted by the memory of his one and only true love.

But now, as the carriage pulled up closer to Rosemoor, Edward felt an unfamiliar sense of urgency gripping him. He clutched the edges of his seat, signalling the horses to move faster. He couldn't be too late. He wouldn't allow it.

When the carriage finally came to a halt outside the Hartley estate, Edward stepped out slowly, his heart pounding in his chest. The house loomed before him, unchanged from the day he had left, but there was a still-ness to it now, an eerie silence that sent a chill through him. He walked up the path, each step heavier than the last, until he reached the front door.

He knocked, his hand shaking slightly as he waited. A few moments passed before the door creaked open, and an old servant ap-peared. The man's eyes widened in recogni-tion, but there was no joy in his expression—only sorrow.

"Mr. Edward," the servant said quietly, his voice thick with emotion. "You've come too late."

Edward's heart stopped. The words hit him like a punch in the face, and for a moment, he couldn't breathe. He shook his head, refusing to believe what he had just heard. "No," he whispered, his voice hoarse. "No, that can't be. I need to see her."

The servant's eyes softened with pity. "I'm sorry, sir," he said gently. "Mrs. Amelia passed just a few hours ago. She went peaceful... but she's gone."

Edward stuttered back, his legs threatening to give in beneath him. The world around him blurred, and a dull, throbbing pain began to build in his chest. It was over. He was too late. He would never see her again, never tell her what had been in his heart all these years. The thought of it was unbearable.

The servant led Edward inside, guiding him through the halls that had once echoed with laughter and life, but now felt cold and empty. They came to a stop in front of a room, the door slightly open. Inside, Amelia lay, pale and still, her face peaceful in death.

Edward stood in the doorway; his breath caught in his throat. He couldn't bring himself to step closer, to see her like this. It felt like a dream—a nightmare from which he would wake any moment. But the reality of her absence settled over him like a heavy cloud.

Slowly, Edward moved toward her, each step heavier than the last. When he finally reached her bedside, he knelt beside her, his shaky hand brushing against her cold cheek. He had imagined this moment so many times, but never like this. He had imagined her eyes lighting up when she saw him, her voice sounding out his name. But now, there was only silence.

Edward's grief came not in an outpouring of tears but in a quiet, overwhelming wave of sorrow that seemed to hollow him from the inside out. He sat by Amelia's side for what felt like hours, his thoughts a mess of memories and regrets. His fingers tracing the lines of her face, as if memorizing them for the last time, so he won't dare forget. She had changed so much, and yet she was still the same Amelia he had loved— and would always love.

His eyes fell to the necklace she held in her hand. It was the one thing he had given her so long ago, a reminder of the love they had shared. The sight of it brought a lump to his throat. Even in death, she had held onto it— onto him. It was a small comfort, but it did nothing to heal the unbearable ache in his heart.

He whispered her name softly, as if she might still hear him. "Amelia..."

But there was no answer. There would never be an answer again.

As the hours went on, Edward remained at her side, lost in his grief, just hoping she would wake up any moment as if she is just taking a long deep nap. He thought of the years they had spent apart; the years he had spent without her. He had tried to move on, tried to find peace in his art, but every painting had been a reflection of her, a piece of his soul poured onto the canvas. He had never stopped loving her, and now, he realized, he never would.

He didn't know how long he stayed there, but eventually, the servant returned, his presence a gentle reminder that time had not stopped, even if he wanted it to.

"Sir," the servant said quietly, "I know this is difficult, but... she's gone now."

Edward nodded, though he didn't trust himself to speak. He rose to his feet, his legs wobbly and unsteady, and with one last look at Amelia, he turned and walked away. Each step felt like a betrayal, as though he were abandoning her all over again. But there was nothing left for him here.

As Edward left the house, the sky above him had darkened, heavy with the clouds of rain. He stood in the garden for a moment, breathing in the fresh air, trying to stable himself. He had come too late. There would be no reunion, no second chance. The love they had shared had died with her.

But even as the weight of his grief threatened to crush him, Edward knew that Amelia would never truly be gone. She lived on in his heart, in his memories and in the paintings that had spread across the world. And in some way, that was enough.

As he turned to leave Rosemoor, Edward knew that he would never forget her. The love they had shared might have been cut short, but it would never die. It would live on in the brushstrokes of his art, in those quiet moments, in the depths of his soul.

It was a love returned too late, but it was a love that would never fade.

Chapter 14: The Canvas of Memory

The wind swept through the cemetery, carrying the scent of moist earth and fallen leaves. Edward stood at Amelia's grave, his heart heavy with grief, his hands shaking as he clutched a bouquet of wildflowers. The stone that carried her name seemed cold, a cruel reminder of the finality of death.

He knelt before the stone, before placing the flowers gently on the grave. His fingers brushed against the engraved letters of her name, his mind racing through his old memories of a time when her laughter had still filled the air, when her eyes had met his with such warmth and promise.

Now, all that was left were echoes of the past and a future that had never came to life.

Edward remained at the graveside for what felt like hours, speaking to Amelia as if she were still there, as if she would somehow hear his words. "I never stopped loving you," he whispered, his voice cracking. "Even when I left... even when you chose him... you were always with me. In every painting, during every thought."

Then came the tears, silently spilling down his cheeks as he longed for the life they never had. The family they could have built, the home they might have shared. All of it, lost to time.

When he could no longer bear the weight of his sorrow, Edward rose slowly to his feet.

His steps were heavy as he left the cemetery, but his mind was racing with only one thought—a desperate need to capture what words could no longer express. He had always poured his soul into his art, and now, he would do the same with his grief.

The next days passed in a blur, as Edward locked himself away in his studio, his emotions guiding his hand across the canvas. He painted with a passion he hadn't felt in years, each stroke of the brush a relief, a tribute, for the love he had lost.

His first painting was of Amelia in her garden, which was her favourite spot in Rosemoor. He remembered her there, her eyes catching the sunlight filtering as she laughed at some small joke, her eyes bright and full of life. He painted her as he remembered her, full of colour and light, a moment engraved in his mind.

But as he worked, the laughter in her eyes faded, and the brightness of the garden dimmed. The painting, once vibrant, became shadowed with melancholy, the joy in her expression replaced with the sorrow that had followed her in life. Edward couldn't stop it—the sadness overtook the canvas, and what began as a memory of happiness became a reflection of the loss that now defined him.

Over the next few weeks, Edward moved from one canvas to the next, painting scene after scene of the life he and Amelia could have shared. Their wedding day, imagining her in white, her face shining with happiness. A quiet evening by the fire, her head resting on his shoulder, the warmth of home surrounding them. Children, their children, playing in the fields of Rosemoor, their laughter filling the air.

But each painting was hinted with sadness. No matter how he tried to imagine a future for them, the past was always there, pulling him back to the cold reality of their separation. The children he painted were never real. The wedding day had never come. The home they could have built was a dream, never to be fulfilled.

The grief poured from his body, becoming stronger with every stroke of his brush, until each painting became representation to the love he had lost. But it wasn't just sorrow he painted. It was love, too. A love that had survived the distance and time, a love that had endured even death.

One day, as he stared at his newest piece— a scene of Amelia standing by the lake where they had once walked—Edward felt a strange sense of peace settle over him. The painting was different from the others. There was still sadness in it, but it wasn't overwhelming. Instead, it felt like acceptance. Amelia stood alone by the water, her face turned toward the horizon, as if she were waiting for something—someone—but there was no despair in her posture. She seemed well, at peace with the life she had lived.

Edward stood before the painting for a long time, his heart swelling with emotion. He realized that moment, that his love for Amelia had never been about possession or the life they could have had. It had always been about the moments they did share, the brief, shining moments of happiness that had changed his life forever.

The paintings transformed into reflections of that realization. They were no longer just about loss—they were about love. A love that had never truly left him, a love that would continue to live on through his art. Each brushstroke was a tribute to her memory, to the life they had dreamed of, and to the love that had shaped them both.

In the weeks that followed, Edward's paintings began to gain attention once more, though now, they carried a new meaning. Critics and admirers spoke of the deep emotions in his work, the sense of loss and longing that seemed to leak from every canvas. But what they saw was only the surface. What Edward knew was that every painting was a piece of his soul, a love letter to the woman who had shaped his life in ways he could never explain.

He continued to visit Amelia's grave, each time bringing a new painting to show her, as if she could see the life he was creating in his memory. And in those moments, standing there in the silence of the cemetery, he felt fulfilled, he felt so close to her—closer than he had ever felt in the years since they had parted.

As he stood there one last time, looking down at the simple gravestone that carried her name, Edward realized that Amelia had never left him. She was in every brushstroke, every colour, every canvas. In his art, their love lived on, immortalized in the beauty of his work.

Chapter 15: The Colours of Forever

The room was covered in the soft glow of afternoon sun, the golden rays filtering through the worn curtains, casting gentle shadows across the cluttered studio. One canvas after another, lined the walls, every surface filled with the portraits and memories of a single woman—Amelia. Her presence seemed to flow through the air, as if she had never truly left.

Edward, now in the body of an old man, sat on his stool, the brush shaking slightly in his frail hand. Though his body had weakened and become worn, his mind remained as sharp as when he first met Amelia all those years ago. His once oak coloured hair was now silver, his face engraved with the lines of time and sorrow. Yet his eyes still held the fire of his youth, the same passion that had driven him to paint countless portraits of Amelia, each one a reflection of the love he had carried for decades.

His latest work—the final masterpiece—lay before him, still unfinished but already breathtaking. It was Amelia as he remembered her, not in her later years, but as she had been when they were young, when their love had blossomed beneath the willow trees of Rosemoor. She was dressed in a simple, flowing gown, her hair gracefully falling down her shoulders, her eyes bright with life and joy. Her smile, soft and full of comfort, seemed to reach out to him, as if inviting him to step into the painting and join her in that timeless moment.

Edward's hand moved slowly, as he added the final touches to her eyes. The rich, deep brown that had once captivated him was now captured on the canvas, alive with the light of youth and hope. He paused for a moment, gazing at the portrait, his heart swelling with a mixture of pride and sorrow. It was perfect—she was perfect. This was how he would remember her, not as the woman who had suffered under the weight of their separation, but as the vibrant, radiant soul he had fallen victim to.

As he stepped back to look at the painting in full size, Edward felt a wave of emotion wash over him. He had painted Amelia so many times, in so many ways, yet this portrait was different. This was not just a reflection of his love—it was a part of the life he never had, the life he had dreamed about but could never realize. In this final painting, she was not burdened by regret or illness. She was free, unfazed by the pain of their separation, a symbol of the love that had outlasted everything else.

The room was quiet. Edward's frail body sank into the chair by his working desk, his breathing slow and steady, though each breath seemed to take more effort than the last. He looked around the studio, his eyes drifting over the countless portraits of Amelia that embellished the walls. Every canvas told a story, each one a chapter of their love—some joyful, some filled with passion, others marked by the sorrow of their parting. Together, they formed the reason of his life, a life that had been made to be linked to hers.

A soft smile crossed his lips as he gazed at the final painting. He felt no fear in that moment, only a deep feeling of peace. He had lived a life of love and loss, but through his art, he had kept her alive with him. Every brushstroke had been a way to hold on to her, to preserve the beauty of what they had shared. And now, as the light of day began to fade, he felt that same beauty wash over him, wrapping him in warmth.

Edward closed his eyes, his thoughts filled with the memories of Amelia—her laughter, her touch, the way she had looked at him that first day in Rosemoor. He could feel her presence, so real, so close, as if she were standing beside him one final time.

The sun dipped below the horizon, casting the studio into nightfall. Edward's breathing slowed, and with one final, peaceful exhale, he slipped into a deep, dreamless sleep. His hands, now still, rested in his lap, the brush having fallen gently to the floor beside the painting.

In the quiet of the room, surrounded by the countless portraits of Amelia, Edward passed from his life. His face was fulfilled, the soft smile still lingering on his lips, as though he had found the peace that he had searched for so long.

The next morning, the light of dawn filtered through the windows, casting a golden ray across the studio. The final painting of Amelia stood at the desk, glowing softly in the morning light. It was a masterpiece, capturing her essence in a way that no words could describe. Her eyes, full of life and love, seemed to watch over the room, a reminder of the connection that had never actually been broken.

Though Edward was gone, his love for Amelia remained, immortalized in the strokes of his brush, in the colours that brought her to life on the canvas. His art, a reflection of his soul, told the story of a love that had outlasted time, distance, and even death.

And as the years passed, Edward's paintings of Amelia became renowned across the world, each one a testament to the enduring power of love. Art lovers and critics alike marvelled at the depth of emotion in his work, unaware that behind every canvas lay a lifetime of devotion, heartbreak, and the longing for a woman who had never truly left him.

In his final masterpiece, Edward had not just captured Amelia's image—he had captured their love, a love that would live on forever, as timeless as the art he left behind.

Epilogue: The Echoes of an Immortal Love

Years after Edward Sinclair's death, his paintings became the subject of great admiration and fascination in the art world. Galleries across the country displayed his work, each piece telling the story that imbodied love and tragedy. Art critics and historians often spoke of Edward's "The Echo of Saudade"—a series of paintings depicting the same woman, captured in various stages of life, always with a hint of longing and unspoken sorrow.

The portraits were hauntingly beautiful, each one filled with a sense of deep, undying love. In some, Amelia was depicted as she was in life—radiant, full of quiet grace. In others, she appeared as a figure from a dream, surrounded by light, her gaze forever turned toward something just out of reach. The most famous of these though, was his final masterpiece, showing the Amelia, that had remained in Edwards mind, full of youth, vibrancy, life, and filled with a joy that had escaped her in her real life.

Visitors to the galleries often found themselves moved to tears, sensing the connection between the artist and his muse. They spoke in hushed tones of the tragic love story that had inspired the collection, a story passed down through the years, growing more touching with each retelling. It was said that Edward had never recovered from losing Amelia, that his heart had been broken beyond repair, and that he had poured every ounce of his love and grief into his art.

In this way, Edward and Amelia's love lived on, immortalized in the brushstrokes and colours that told their story. Their love, though tragic and unfulfilled in life, became eternal in art.

And so, in the galleries where his paintings hung, Edward and Amelia were together once more, forever bound by the love that had defined their lives. In every portrait, in every delicate line and shade of colour, their love whispered through the ages, a reminder that true love, no matter how tragic, is never truly lost.

And perhaps, somewhere beyond the canvas, beyond this world, Edward and Amelia were together once more, their love finally free to flourish, unburdened by the sorrows of the past.

The End.

About the Author

Elysia is a 14-year-old high school student living in Austria, with a heart full of stories and a love for all things vintage. A true romantic at heart, she finds inspiration in timeless love stories, especially the real-life story of the Titanic, a subject she is deeply passionate about. When she is not writing, Elysia paints, sings, and dances, bringing beauty to the world in every form she can. The Echo Of Saudade is her heartfelt debut, filled with emotion, imagination, and the timeless magic of love.